Phineas stared at the screen as a character who looked like Buford appeared in the game.

"How did you get your face in there?" Phineas asked curiously.

Using the video game's built-in camera, Buford snapped a photo of Phineas.

Suddenly Phineas
WAS IN THE GAME, too!

   Meanwhile, Phineas and Ferb's older sister, Candace, was getting ready to go to a dance with her friend Jeremy. But what if her brothers did something to ruin her special date?

   "What are you guys up to?" she demanded.

   "Playing a video game," Phineas replied. That gave him an idea!